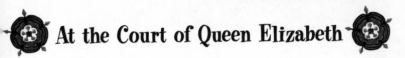

Sir Walter's Last Chance

by Karen Wallace

Illustrated by Jane Cope

W

FRANKLIN WATTS

LONDON•SYDNEY

First published in 2000 by Franklin Watts
96 Leonard Street, London EC2A 4XD

Text © Karen Wallace 2000

The right of Karen Wallace to be identified
as the Author of this Work has been asserted
by her in accordance with the Copyright,
Designs and Patents Act, 1988

Editor: Louise John
Designer: Jason Anscomb
Consultants: Dr Anne Millard, BA Hons, Dip Ed, PhD
             Alison Toplis, Fashion Historian

A CIP catalogue record for this book
is available from the British Library.

ISBN   0 7496 3758 7 (hbk)
        0 7496 3975 X (pbk)

Dewey Classification 942.05

Printed in Great Britain

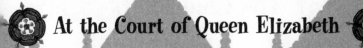

Sir Walter's Last Chance

by Karen Wallace

Illustrated by Jane Cope

W
FRANKLIN WATTS
LONDON•SYDNEY

The Characters

Old Ma Knucklebone

Sir Walter Raleigh

Mary Marchbank

Bishop of Bellchurch

Queen Elizabeth

Matilda, Lady Mouthwater

Toby Crumble

Earl Inkblot

Midshipman Bob

CONTENTS

✿ CHAPTER ONE ✿
The Customer Comes First

Old Ma Knucklebone peered at the boy's thin grimy face.

She grabbed his bony shoulders. "You ain't tellin' lies, is ya?"

"No, Ma'am."

"What's yer name?"

"Percy, Ma'am," croaked the boy. "I takes messages for Sir Walter Raleigh."

Percy shivered. He had never seen such a strange-looking hag in all his life.

Even her hovel looked more like a cave. Or an animal's den. Old skins hung on the wall and there were bits of bones and feathers everywhere. In one damp corner a pot bubbled over a low fire.

Percy wrinkled his nose. It smelt disgusting.

Old Ma Knucklebone tightened her grip on Percy's shoulders. "Cos if I goes all the way to the Tower of London and Sir Walter Raleigh ain't expecting me –"

Percy felt her strong hands turn him round.

In front of his eyes was a large bottle packed with dried toads. Old Ma Knucklebone opened the top and pulled one out.

For one horrible moment, Percy thought she was
going to stuff it into his mouth.

"Why would I come all this way if I was lyin'?"
said Percy, quickly. He twisted out of her grasp.
"Besides, he won't pay me till you shows up."

Old Ma Knucklebone chuckled. "That's more
like it!" she said, as she absent-mindedly nibbled on
the dried toad. "So what's a fancy man like Sir
Walter Raleigh wanting with the likes of me?"

"He says you're his last chance to get out of the
Tower of London," said Percy.

"What's he done?" Old Ma Knucklebone pulled another toad from the jar.

"He married a pretty girl without the Queen's permission."

"That was foolish of him," murmured Old Ma Knucklebone. She swallowed the toad. "The Queen don't like her courtiers marrying. Especially if the girl is prettier than 'er."

"I hears that ain't difficult." Percy pulled a face. "Some say the Queen's bald as a coot and wrinkled as a prune."

But Old Ma Knucklebone wasn't listening; she was busy stuffing bits of skin and bone and pots of grease into a large sack. No point in trudging all the way to to the Tower unprepared. Besides, things were slow in the spells and potions business and if she got this job right, it might lead to others.

Old Ma Knucklebone hefted the sack over her shoulder and pulled the door open. "Let's go," she said.

Daylight flooded into the room and Old Ma Knucklebone blinked. Suddenly she remembered she hadn't changed her cap or her clothes for at least a few months.

And Sir Walter Raleigh was a new customer.

Old Ma Knucklebone dumped the sack down on the floor. No point in worrying about the clothes. She only had one set, anyway. But she was sure there was another cap underneath a pile of foxtails in the corner.

"Tell 'im I'll be there this sunset," muttered Old Ma Knucklebone, as she pinned one of the foxtails to the cap, for luck.

"Promise?" said Percy.

Sir Walter Raleigh was paying him a penny and that would buy him enough food to last a week!

Old Ma Knucklebone fixed Percy with a beady eye. "You won't go hungry, lad. Don't worry, you'll get your penny."

Percy gasped. How could she have known that? Maybe she was a witch after all.

He turned and ran as fast as he could into the crowded street.

THE TOWER OF LONDON

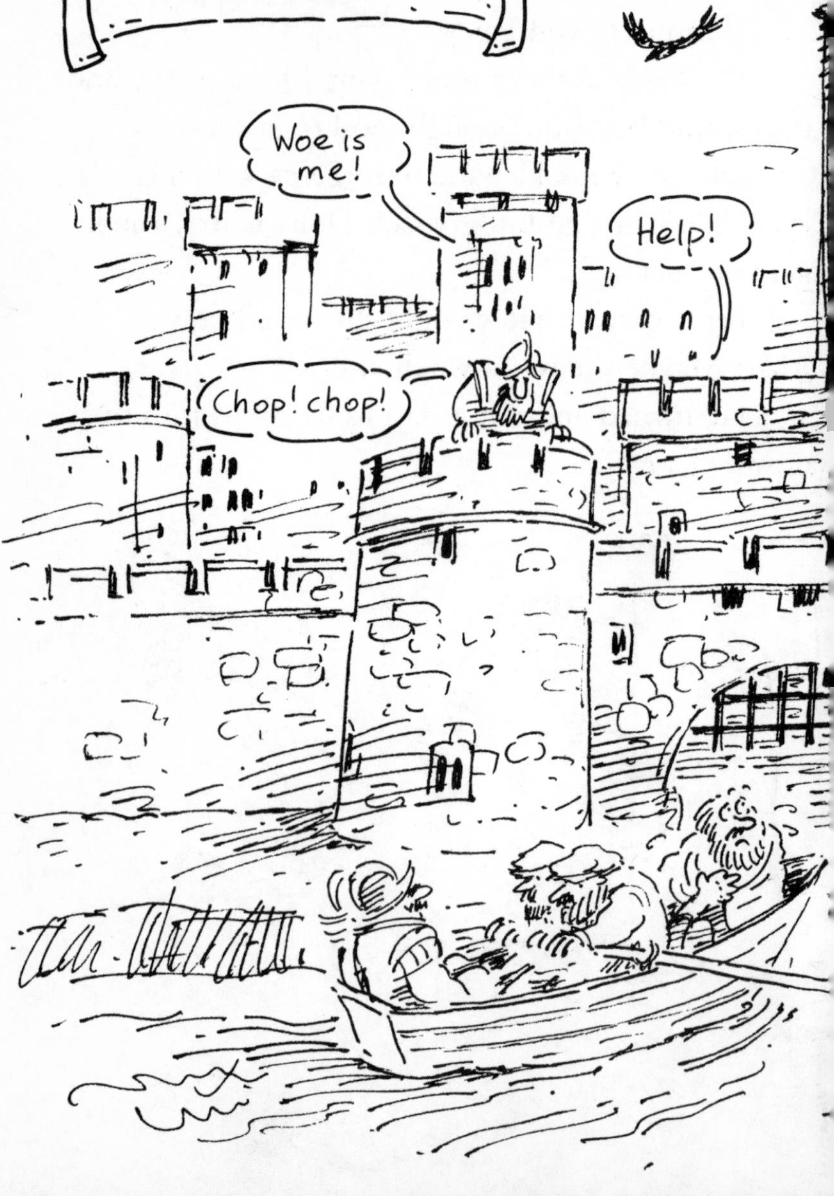

Inside the Tower of London, Sir Walter Raleigh sat at a high wooden desk and stared at the pile of papers that lay on the floor at his feet.

Each piece of paper was a copy of a letter he had written to Queen Elizabeth I. Each letter begged her, in as many different ways as he could think of, to set him free.

Sir Walter groaned and looked across to the other side of the room.

Another pile of papers lay by the door. Each one was a letter written by him. Each one had 'Return to Sender' scrawled across the top in the Queen's handwriting.

Sir Walter closed his eyes and rubbed his hand across his high broad forehead. It was almost impossible to believe that he had once been the Queen's favourite at her Court. Had he really worn pearls in his ears and a pleated white ruff as wide a cartwheel? Had he really paid thirty pounds for a jewelled hat band?

Sir Walter opened his eyes and shook his head. It seemed impossible, but it was true. And now his career was ruined because he had married a pretty girl.

Sir Walter pulled a face. It just wasn't fair. Especially since the Queen was as bald as a coot and as wrinkled as a prune!

Outside, the setting sun turned the clouds pink and orange. Something huffed and puffed and scratched at the door. It sounded like a huge rat.

Sir Walter jumped up.

"Who's there?" he called.

Instinctively he put his hand to his sword but, of course, no weapon hung from his belt.

"It's only me," cackled a voice. The door opened and a horrible smell filled the room.

"Old Ma Knucklebone come to see you, Sir."

Sir Walter Raleigh gasped. Then he clenched his jaw muscles to stop his mouth dropping open.

The lumpy hag in front of him had a face like a bloated squirrel. She wore a filthy grey dress with an apron that was black and green and covered with mustard-coloured crusty bits. A lucky foxtail hung from the greasy cap on her head.

Sir Walter felt his stomach turn over. He took a deep breath and looked away.

"You is expectin' me, in't ya?" said Old Ma Knucklebone anxiously.

"Uh, indeed, I am, dear lady," stuttered Sir Walter. He had to pull himself together. This woman really was his last chance.

Sir Walter bowed and dragged over a chair. "Pray be seated," he muttered.

"Not I, Sir." Old Ma Knucklebone looked suspiciously at the chair. "I never sits when I'm working. You never knows as who's been sitting down before ya." She grinned a toothless grin.

Sir Walter was so overcome by the smell in the room, he sat down on the chair himself.

"There now," murmured Old Ma Knucklebone. She laid a grimy hand on his shoulder. "I expects it's yer nerves."

Sir Walter made a gagging noise. It wasn't his nerves. He thought he was going to be sick.

He raised his hand and tried feebly to wave Old Ma Knucklebone away. "Please, please —"

Old Ma Knucklebone grinned again. "I'll roll the bones now," she chuckled. "Don't you worry, Sir, soon you'll be out of here."

Then she reached into a leather pouch that hung from her belt and threw a handful of bones across the top of the wooden desk.

"The bones never lie, My Lord."

❀ CHAPTER TWO ❀
A Cure for Toothache

"It's all Sir Walter Raleigh's fault," muttered Queen Elizabeth I. She touched the bandage that was wrapped around her swollen jaw. "I didn't have toothache before –" She scrawled 'Return to Sender' across the front of a letter and threw it on the floor.

"BEFORE HE BETRAYED ME!" she bellowed at the top of her voice.

"Calm yourself, My Lady," murmured the Bishop of Bellchurch. "'Tis the toothache that is making you angry."

Godfrey, Earl of Inkblot, stepped forward and bowed. "Her Majesty's pain is a torment to us all," he said in the most soothing voice he could manage. "If you would only allow the surgeon –"

A man in a black apron stepped forward.

"To pull it out?" shrieked the Queen.

"Yes, Your Majesty," whispered the Earl of Inkblot.

"What if it hurts?" yelled the Queen.

"It won't hurt, My Lady," said the Bishop of Bellchurch.

A nasty gleam appeared in the Queen's eyes.

At the other side of the room, her maid Mary Marchbank held her breath. She knew all about that gleam. It was a sure sign that the Queen was up to no good.

The Queen stood up and fixed the Bishop with a cold stare. "Prove it," she said.

At first the Bishop didn't understand. "But, Your Majesty," he murmured. "I don't have toothache."

"So what," snarled the Queen, "you have teeth, don't you?"

The Bishop of Bellchurch went white and put his hand to his mouth.

"But, Your Majesty –"

"But, Your Majesty – " mimicked the Queen. "Just sit down."

She glared at the surgeon. "Take out his tooth so that I can see it doesn't hurt."

The room went silent. As if in slow motion the surgeon held up a pair of long narrow pliers. The Bishop's whiskery nose twitched uncontrollably. He looked exactly like a frightened rabbit.

As fast as she could, Mary Marchbank glided across the room to the fireplace. Inside the stone hearth was a deep shelf where she always kept a bowl of hot water.

She set the bowl on a table. Then she dropped in the huge bunch of marjoram she had picked in the garden that morning.

The surgeon was bending and looking into the Bishop's open mouth when the Queen turned and sniffed the air.

"What's that *wonderful* smell?" she murmured as a sleepy look came into her eyes.

"Soothing marjoram, Your Majesty," said Mary Marchbank softly. She bowed and put the steaming bowl as near to the Queen's nose as she dared. "It's your favourite."

"So it is," sighed the Queen. She breathed in deeply and leaned back on her throne. "I would willingly spend my days in a field of marjoram."

Mary saw her chance. "Shall I show these gentlemen out, Your Majesty?" she said gently.

"What a *good* idea, Mary," murmured the Queen sleepily. "We don't want them here, anyway."

Mary never saw a man move so fast. The Bishop of Bellchurch was out of his chair and through the door in one quick movement.

He just had time to press a sweaty coin in Mary's hand. Then he was gone!

***

27

A TUDOR KITCHEN

"What will happen when the Queen wakes up?" Toby Crumble wiped tears of laughter from his eyes.

Toby was a cook in the Queen's kitchen. He and Mary were old friends.

"That's why I came to see you," said Mary. She looked around the huge kitchen with its gleaming pots and pans. Everywhere people were chopping and slicing and preparing food for the Queen's supper.

"She's fed up with gruel and she can only eat mush because of her toothache," explained Mary. "What can I give her?"

"What about a new kind of soup?" suggested Toby

"I've just invented one called Minestrone."

Mary sighed. She didn't have
the heart to tell Toby what the Queen
had done with the Chicken Noodle
soup he had sent up earlier.

What's more she felt terribly
sorry for the person who had been
underneath the Queen's
window at the time.

"She's fed up with soup, too," said Mary. "She needs something completely new and tasty."

Toby shrugged. "She's tasted every spice and herb in my kitchen," he said. "There's nothing new to be had."

Mary bit her lip. "Poor Sir Walter," she murmured, "as long as the Queen has toothache, he'll stay in prison."

"Perhaps there's something we can do —" said Toby thoughtfully.

Only that morning, he'd heard two stable lads gossiping. They were grooming horses and it was hard work because the horses and their riders had come all the way from Devon.

According to the stable lads, one of Sir Walter Raleigh's ships had just sailed into Plymouth from the New World.

A light came into Toby's eyes. Sir Walter's last ship had been packed with all kinds of tasty, new spices. Mary stared at Toby's face. "What is it? What are you thinking?"

When Toby told her, a huge grin spread across Mary Marchbank's face.

Then she frowned. "But how can I find out what the ship's cargo is?"

"Ask Sir Walter himself," said Toby. "You told me the Queen sends all his letters back. You could be the messenger."

Mary Marchbank threw up her hands. "Toby Crumble," she cried. "You're a genius!"

CHAPTER THREE
A Most Peculiar Recipe

Sir Walter Raleigh stared at the smelly pile of bones that lay all over his desk. What he had just heard sounded like the ravings of a lunatic.

"Could you say that again, please?"

"You must boil stones. She who eats of the boiled stones will free you from prison." Old Ma Knucklebone prodded a particularly nasty looking bone. "See, there it is as clear as day."

Old Ma Knucklebone
held out a grimy hand.
"One sovereign, please."

Sir Walter made a gagging sound. "You must be joking! One sovereign to tell me to boil stones?"

Old Ma Knucklebone fixed him with her bloodshot eyes. "One sovereign."

Reluctantly, Sir Walter Raleigh placed a shiny gold coin in the outstretched hand in front of him.

He had never felt so miserable in all his life. He felt sure that he would be locked away in the Tower for ever and never see his pretty young wife again.

"You'll see your wife before the moon's full," cackled Old Ma Knucklebone. "The bones never lie."

Sir Walter Raleigh gasped. How could she have known what he was thinking? But, before he could ask her, Old Ma Knucklebone was gone.

***

TUDOR TREASURES

Dubloons
and jewels
from Spain.

Brandy
and fine
wines
from
France.

Mary Marchbank stood in front of the heavy prison door and wrapped her woollen cloak tightly around her. It wasn't that she was cold but there was something about the Tower of London that made her shiver.

At that moment, the door creaked open on its huge iron hinges. Mary jumped back. A face she hadn't seen for ages appeared in front of her.

It looked just like a
bloated squirrel.

Old Ma Knucklebone
leaned forward and whispered
in Mary's ear.

"'Tis the stones will save
'im, mark my words, lass."

And, without another
word, she slipped out into
the murky evening.

"State your business,"
boomed a voice in Mary's ear.

A black-bearded giant of
a man stepped forward.

"I'm the gaoler of the
Tower of London and I don't
like to be kept waiting."

Mary blushed and
curtseyed. "I'm lady's maid
to the Queen," she muttered.
"I've a letter for Sir Walter."

The gaoler laughed
loudly and showed off his
rotten teeth.

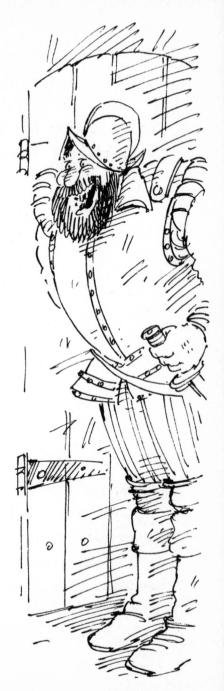

"Not another one!" He held out his hand. "I'll take it."

"No!" Mary blushed again. "I mean, please, I must give it to him myself."

"There's a penny to be had for every letter handed to Sir Walter," snarled the gaoler. "And that penny is mine."

And before Mary could stop him, he snatched the letter out of her hand and slammed the door shut in her face. Mary was distraught.

"Is this where I can find Sir Walter Raleigh?"

Mary turned.

A man with a deeply tanned face and an earring in his ear was standing behind her.

"I've come all
the way from Devon
and I'm mighty tired."

Mary stared at the
man's face. He wore a spotted
handkerchief around his neck and leather boots
that were stained with salt water.

An extraordinary thought occurred to her.

"Were you a sailor on Sir Walter's ship, Sir?"
The man grinned and bowed. "Bosun Bob at your
service," he said.

Mary couldn't believe her luck. "Would you tell
me what your ship was carrying?"

The man frowned. "I've had orders only to tell
Sir Walter, lass."

"I ask for the Queen's sake," said Mary quickly. "She's sick with the toothache and off her food."

At the mention of the Queen, Bosun Bob straightened the spotted kerchief around his neck.

"We carried pepper, cloves, cinnamon, mace and nutmeg," he said, counting his fingers. "And also jewels, amber and musk."

Mary's heart sank. There was nothing new and tasty there. "Anything else?" she asked.

Bob shrugged. "Only sacks of strange stones which the natives grow in the New World."

Mary frowned. "But stones don't grow."

"These ones do," replied Bob, "and hard and disgusting they are, too!"

"Do you have any of these *stones* with you?" asked Mary slowly.

Bosun Bob reached into his sailors' bag and opened out a brown paper parcel. He handed Mary what looked like a dirty brown stone.

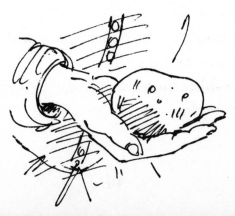

Mary rolled the strange stone around in her hand. Stubby white roots sprouted out all over it. It looked like the last thing in the world that would help a toothache. Or indeed be something new and tasty for the Queen to eat.

What had Old Ma Knucklebone said? "'*Tis the stones will save 'im.*"

Mary bit her lip. Perhaps Toby Crumble would know what to do.

"May I borrow your stones?" she said. "I'll see they are returned to Sir Walter."

"You can have them, lass," said Bosun Bob. "If they will help the Queen, they might help my master get out of this place."

❀ CHAPTER FOUR ❀
Off With His Head

"Your Majesty!" cried Godfrey, Earl of Inkblot.
"A toothache is no reason to have a man beheaded!"

"It is if his name is Walter Raleigh," snarled the
Queen. She held up a mirror and looked at her face.
One side was the size of a football.

"Summon the clerk!" bellowed the Queen.
"I shall dictate the order."

"The clerk is sick with the boils, Your Majesty,"

whispered Matilda, Lady Mouthwater. Her hands flapped nervously at her side.

"Then you shall write it yourself," snapped the Queen. "Such busy hands as yours need work."

"But my writing is slow and mean," cried Matilda, Lady Mouthwater. "I am not practised in such things."

Mary Marchbank looked up. A nasty gleam had come into the Queen's eye – again!

"Then it can make no difference if you lose your hands along with Sir Walter's head," she said.

Matilda, Lady Mouthwater gasped and slumped to the floor.

"Your Majesty!" cried Godfrey, Earl of Inkblot. "The Lady Mouthwater has fainted."

Queen Elizabeth I stuck out her bottom lip.

"It was only a jest," she muttered in a sulky voice.

"Thank goodness!" Godfrey, Earl of Inkblot pulled out his handkerchief and wiped his brow.

"Send for a *new* clerk!" snapped the Queen. Another nasty look flickered across her face. "And Sir Walter Raleigh! He will watch me sign the order."

Mary Marchbank's stomach turned over. She had do something and do it fast.

She sensed that somehow the Queen's toothache, Sir Walter's freedom and the strange stones from the New World were all connected.

But how?

Mary backed out of the room and ran all the way to the kitchen.

She hoped against hope that Toby Crumble had the answer but the kitchen was empty.

Mary's heart banged like a hammer in her chest. Where was Toby? And more importantly, where were the stones she had given him to look after?

At that moment, Toby crept into the room.

His face was white and creased. It was almost as if he had been crying.

"It wasn't my fault, Mary!" he blurted. "The cat did it." Toby stared wildly at the great hearth.

"I lined them up on the shelf to see if they

would ripen and, and –" He put his hands over his face. "Oh Mary! I'm so sorry."

"What happened?" cried Mary.

"The cat knocked the stones into the cooking pot," said Toby in a hollow voice. "They're ruined, they're *mush.*"

"Which is exactly what you want to eat if you have a toothache!"

Mary and Toby spun round.

Old Ma Knucklebone was hobbling across the flagstone floor towards them.

"Don't just stand there like a pair of daft boobies," she cried. "The Queen is in such a bad mood, she has ordered Sir Walter Raleigh's execution."

Mary's hands flew to her face. "Oh, no!"

"He's on his way to see her sign the order," said Old Ma Knucklebone.

She banged her fist on a wooden table. "We have to cure the Queen's toothache before she picks up her pen."

Old Ma Knucklebone reached into her pocket and pulled out a handful of cloves wrapped in a linen cloth. "Now do what I tell you."

Mary nodded quickly.

"Pound these to a pulp and place them on the Queen's sore tooth," said Old Ma Knucklebone.

Mary grabbed the cloth. "What if it doesn't work?"

"It'll work. Them cloves is soaked in a special potion."

"But what about the stones?" asked Toby. "Aren't they the cure to the Queen's toothache?"

Old Ma Knucklebone shook her head. "The stones have nothing to do with curing the Queen's toothache." She paused. "The stones will free Sir Walter from the Tower of London just like the bones foretold."

"But how?" said Mary.

"Leave that to me," answered Old Ma Knucklebone sharply. "You see to your mistress."

Mary turned and ran from the kitchen.

Old Ma Knucklebone wiped her hands on her filthy apron. "Now Toby, let's have a look at this cooking pot of yours."

CHAPTER FIVE
Something New and Tasty

Godfrey, Earl of Inkblot couldn't believe his eyes.

The Bishop of Bellchurch was convinced it was a miracle.

Half an hour after Mary Marchbank had placed the wad of crushed cloves on the Queen's bad tooth, the ache had disappeared and her swollen jaw had gone back to normal.

By the time Sir Walter Raleigh was shown into the royal room, the air was filled with the soothing smell of marjoram and the Queen was playing a game of cards with Matilda, Lady Mouthwater.

It was as if her toothache had never happened.

"Ah, Sir Walter," murmured the Queen. "How lovely to see you."

"The pleasure is mine, Your Majesty," croaked Sir Walter. He had been told he was to witness his own execution order.

He looked nervously around the room. If this was a trap, it was a devilishly clever one.

The Queen waved a delicate white hand, "Will you join us for supper?"

"J-j-join you for supper, Your Majesty?" stammered Sir Walter.

"That's what I said, didn't I?" snapped the Queen. "It is supper time, isn't it?"

She sat up and clapped her hands. "Mary Marchbank! Bring food for myself and Sir Walter."

A nasty gleam came into her eye. "And make sure it's something new and tasty."

***

Down in the kitchen, Old Ma Knucklebone stuck her finger into a bowl of fluffy, white stuff. She sucked it thoughtfully. "More butter and lots of pepper."

"What shall we call it?" asked Toby as he put a lump of butter on top of the white pile.

"How about soft stones?" said Old Ma Knucklebone.

"Doesn't sound right. How about mash?" Toby laughed. "After all that's what we did to the stones."

Old Ma Knucklebone grinned. "Mash it is. Unless Sir Raleigh knows the proper name. It's his discovery after all."

At that moment, Mary Marchbank ran into the

kitchen. "The Queen wants her supper," she gasped, "and it has to be something new and tasty!"

"Excellent!" chuckled Old Ma Knucklebone. "That's exactly what she'll get."

Old Ma Knucklebone raised her eyebrows. "Has her toothache gone?"

Mary nodded.

"Has Sir Walter arrived?"

Mary nodded again.

"Has he been asked to stay for supper?"

Mary gasped. "How did you –?"

Old Ma Knucklebone winked. "Never you mind."

She picked up the plate of fluffy white mash. "Take this up to Her Majesty. Say it comes with the compliments of Sir Walter Raleigh." She grabbed a pepper grinder from the shelf. "And don't forget to give her the pepper as that's his doing, too!"

Mary stared at the plate in her hands. "You mean these are the stones that fell in the pot?"

Old Ma Knucklebone grinned. "The very same. And I'll bet sixpence, Sir Walter will be a free man before the evening's out."

***

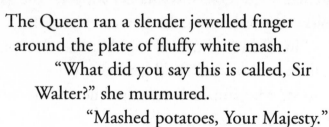

The Queen ran a slender jewelled finger
around the plate of fluffy white mash.

"What did you say this is called, Sir
Walter?" she murmured.

"Mashed potatoes, Your Majesty."
The Queen popped the last
of the mash into her
mouth and turned to
Sir Walter Raleigh.

"We like your, um,
mashed potatoes, Sir."

"I am honoured,
Your Majesty," he
replied.

The Queen snapped
her fingers at the clerk
waiting nervously

"Write this down."
Sir Walter's face went
completely grey.

A smile flickered
on the Queen's lips.

"From this day on, all potatoes shall belong to the crown."

Sir Walter bowed.

"In return, Sir Walter Raleigh shall be freed from the Tower of London."

Sir Walter fell on his knees.

The Queen picked up the empty plate. "Those are my orders —" a nasty gleam came into her eye, "as long as there are seconds."

Sir Walter Raleigh's eyes were round with terror.

Mary Marchbank thought she was going to faint.

Suddenly, there was a scratching sound and the door opened.

Old Ma Knucklebone was standing in the doorway, grinning and holding a huge dish of fluffy mashed potatoes!

❀ NOTES ❀
At the Court of Queen Elizabeth (How it really was!)

Sir Walter's Last Chance is a made-up story but it is a story based on real historical facts. Here are some of those facts:

The Queen and the Tower of London

Elizabeth I had a particular dislike of the Tower because she had been held there as a suspected traitor by her sister, Queen Mary. However, it was much used as a prison and as a place of banishment during her own reign.

Sir Walter Raleigh

Sir Walter was a great favourite of the Queen before he married. He became very rich because she gave him the sole right to sell woollen cloth, sweet white wine and the playing card.

Bess Throckmorton

Bess Throckmorton was a lady of the Queen's Chamber so the Queen was particularly furious when she secretly married Raleigh. She banished Bess to the country and sent Raleigh to the Tower.

Elizabethan money

The value of money has increased by roughly five hundred times since the Tudor era. Elizabethan coins were very different. There were farthings, halfpennies, groats, angels and sovereigns. Percy's penny would have been worth about £2.00 in today's money. It would have been enough for him to buy bread for a whole week.

1 penny = £2.00
1 shilling = £25.00
£1 = £500.00

Dental Care

Throughout her life, the Queen suffered
from toothache and eventually all her teeth
went black. She brushed her teeth with a
mixture of white wine, vinegar and honey
and cleaned them with special 'tooth cloths'.
She had many gold toothpicks listed
among her possessions.

The Bishop of London

The Queen really did order the Bishop of London to have one of his own teeth pulled so that she could see it didn't hurt!

Fancy Food

Elizabethans liked decorative food. They were particularly fond of fancy pies in different shapes. Often, live birds were placed in a cooked game pie at the last minute to create a spectacle when the pie was cut open. In private, the Queen preferred plain food and only drank weak beer. She often ate with only a few attendants.